Dedication
To Sophia
Who fills my heart with joy

"Who, Nana Bear, Who?": A Book About Patriotism

©2023 Bonnie Mackey. All Rights Reserved. No part of this publication may be reproduced, stored in a retrieval system or transmitted in any form by any means electronic, mechanical, or photocopying, recording or otherwise without the permission of the author.

ISBN: 978-1-7336015-3-5

Printed in the United States

"Who, Nana Bear, Who?"

A Book About Patriotism

Written by Bonnie Mackey

Illustrated by Catherine R. Hamilton

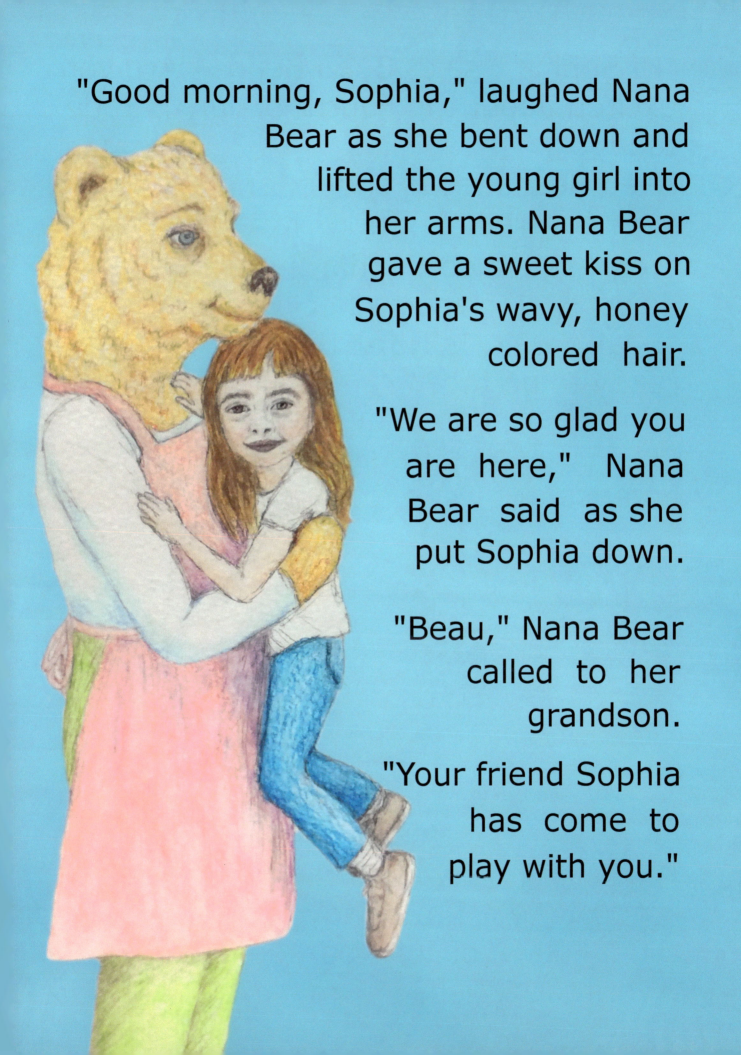

"Good morning, Sophia," laughed Nana Bear as she bent down and lifted the young girl into her arms. Nana Bear gave a sweet kiss on Sophia's wavy, honey colored hair.

"We are so glad you are here," Nana Bear said as she put Sophia down.

"Beau," Nana Bear called to her grandson.

"Your friend Sophia has come to play with you."

"Hi Sophia," said Beau Bear. "Are you excited about the Fourth of July parade today?"

Beau Bear's eyes shone, and his boyish grin covered his furry face.

"Yes!" squealed Sophia, jumping up and down and clapping her hands. "I can't wait. Is Nana Bear ready to go too?"

Nana Bear popped into the room, waving a Betsy Ross American flag.

"Of course, I'm ready," she cheered. "The Fourth of July parade is one of my favorite things!"

"Do you want to hold a flag, Sophia?" asked Nana Bear, as she bent down to gather a handful of small American flags.

Sophia took one flag and held it to her heart.

"I learned to say the Pledge of Allegiance to our American flag in my kindergarten class last year at school," said Sophia.

"Oh, yes, that is very patriotic," said Nana Bear.

"Today, on July Fourth, Americans can display our patriotism by waving flags, attending parades, and enjoying our freedoms with our family at a backyard cookout," explained Nana Bear.

Beau Bear was jumping up and cheering in front of the big window.

Outside of Nana Bear's home, the siren from a huge, red fire truck screamed.

"The parade is starting," clapped Sophia, as she put her hands over her ears to stifle the loud sounds coming from the siren.

"Quick!!" exclaimed Nana Bear, as she grabbed Sophia's small hand in her right paw and Beau's furry paw in her left paw. "Let's run down to the road to get closer."

Sophia turned to Beau and said, "Oh, oh, oh, look who is coming first in our patriotic parade," as she pointed to a large boat on a flatbed truck.

"He was our very first President!!" shouted Sophia, "and he helped our country get off to a great start."

Beau Bear looked puzzled.

"Who, Nana Bear, who?" he said as he waved at the young boy on the float.

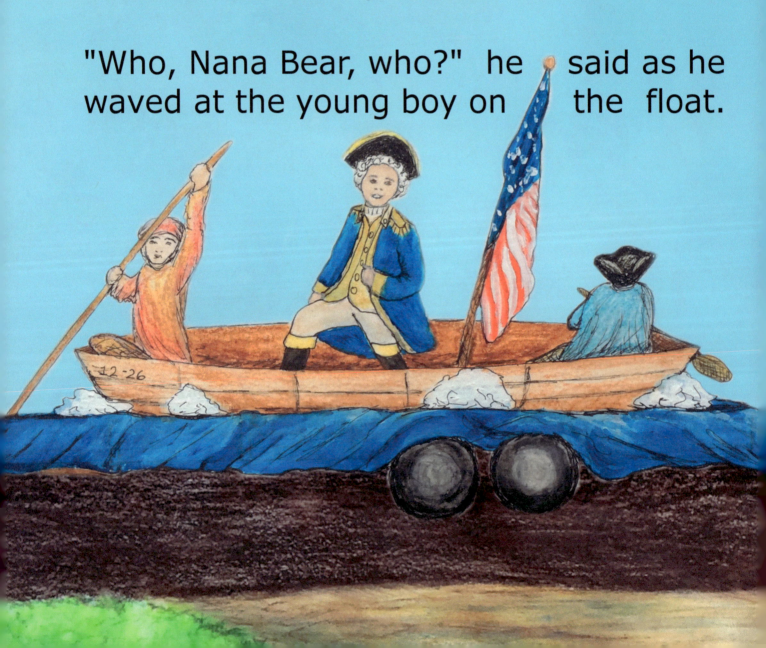

Nana Bear's face beamed with pride as she replied very softly.

"He is George Washington, and he represents LIBERTY."

"I like having liberty, don't you, Sophia?" asked Beau Bear.

"Yes, yes, yes!!" exclaimed Sophia. "Having liberty means you are free to make your own choices about yourself and what you want to do when you grow up. We are lucky we have so many choices of careers and lifestyles."

"I want to be a tall, big bear when I grow up," said Beau Bear as he stood on his toes to be as tall as he could be.

Sophia giggled. Her head bounced up and down as tiny peals of laughter danced from her mouth with short, soft movements.

"Washington Crossing the Delaware" by Emanuel Leutze, 1851.

On Christmas Day, 1776, George Washington led soldiers of the Continental Army across the icy Delaware River in a surprise attack. The bravery of Washington and his men gave America a victory and boosted morale in the battle for America's independence from England.

The second float rolled in front of Sophia, Beau Bear, and Nana Bear. Sophia gasped at the beautiful Native American girl standing tall in front of several tree-covered mountains.

"Oh, she looks so pretty," sighed Sophia.

"Who, Nana Bear, Who?" asked Beau Bear, as he stared up at the girl holding her young infant.

"That brave, courageous lady is Sacajawea," laughed Nana Bear. "She led Lewis and Clark on their journey westward over the Blue Ridge Mountains. Because she grew up near the mountains, she was familiar with all the trails and roads westward. Sacajawea, along with Lewis and Clark, expanded our country and gave us more land for Americans to settle on, grow crops, and have families. She represents ADVENTURE."

Beau Bear turned to Sophia and said, "What does adventure mean?"

"Wait, I have to think," murmured Sophia, with her hand under her chin.

"Remember when we got up early one morning, packed our backpacks, and walked on the new trails we had never been on before? We were both nervous and excited at the same time, because we didn't know what we would see or encounter. That is an adventure."

Detail, "Lewis and Clark at Three Forks" by Edgar S. Paxson, 1912.

Sacajawea, with her husband and baby, were guides for the Lewis and Clark expedition that explored the recently purchased Louisiana Territory. From 1804 to 1806, they traveled from the Great Plains to the Pacific Ocean and back.

"Quick," said Nana Bear. "Turn and look who is coming now in our July Fourth parade of patriotic people."

Coming down the road was a smaller float, carrying an old, stained rocking chair. Rocking back and forth was a small, huddled figure of an African-American girl, holding a faded, paper map in her hands.

"Oh, my goodness," whispered Nana Bear, "She looks so tiny, but so brave."

"Who, Nana Bear, who?" asked Beau, staring straight into the wrinkled, worn face from the float.

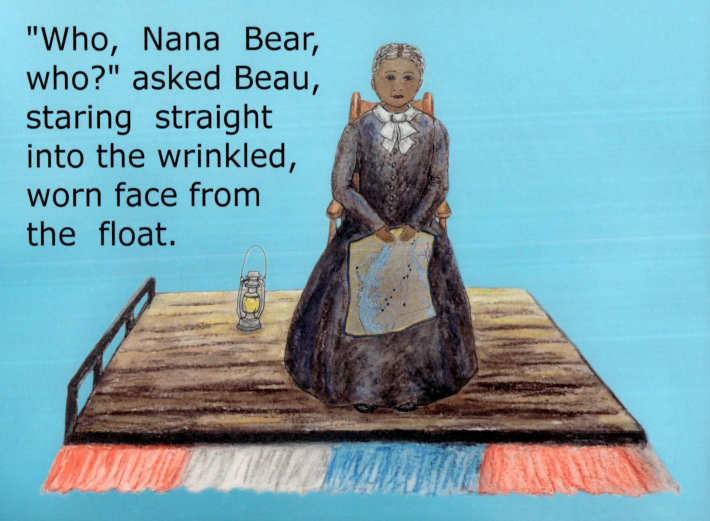

"This brave lady is Harriet Tubman. She helped to free so many slaves by establishing a network of good, kind folks who would guide the slaves to freedom."

"Harriet Tubman represents COURAGE."

Sophia was jumping up and down.

She said, "I know, I know. That was called the Underground Railroad. My first grade teacher read us a story about it."

"Courage," pondered Beau Bear, looking at Sophia.

"Hmmm," he said.

"Courage is overcoming fear and anxiety. Remember when I was afraid and anxious to ride my skateboard for the first time?

You and Nana Bear both reassured me that I could ride it. I overcame my fear and rode it, and now I know what fun it can be."

Harriet Tubman, 1911, Library of Congress

Between 1810 and 1863, the Underground Railroad helped to guide several thousand enslaved people to freedom. Harriet Tubman, the most famous 'conductor' on the Underground Railroad, traveled through many dangerous journeys to lead groups of slaves to safer locations.

With a loud honk of the horn, another flatbed truck, decorated with American flags and a large airplane, rode by. Standing beside one of the wings of the plane was a girl, holding a rivet tool against the airplane's fuselage.

"Oh, my goodness, she was amazing," said Sophia in a voice quite husky with awe and disbelief.

"Who, Nana Bear, who?" said Beau Bear.

Nana Bear smiled a very large grin.

"That courageous and smart lady is Rosie the Riveter. She learned how to build airplanes during World War II to get them ready for the pilots to fly. She used tools to fasten the rivets that held the airplanes together. She represents INGENUITY."

Hundreds of thousands of solid-shank, button-head rivets held WWII aircraft together.

"Huh?" said Beau Bear with a very puzzled look on his cub face.

Sophia laughed.

"Well," she said slowly, "let's ask Nana Bear about ingenuity."

"What does ingenuity mean?" shouted Beau Bear and Sophia in unison.

"That is a good question," Nana Bear grinned. "Let me think."

"Remember, Beau, when you were making a Christmas card for your preschool teacher? You couldn't find any glue to paste the sparkling ornaments on the green tree you had colored on the front of the card. So you used ingenuity to come up with a different, but fun, way to keep the ornaments on the tree. Do you remember what you used?"

Beau's round, tan face beamed with excitement.

"Yes, yes! I used some red Christmas ribbon to tie the ornaments to the tree. But first, I had to use the hole puncher to make holes in the green tree and then I was able to push the ribbons that held the ornaments into the holes and tie them in the back of the card."

Nana Bear's smile was as wide as the flatbed truck that had carried Rosie the Riveter.

"Brilliant," she said. "That is ingenuity- being able to use your mind and your hands to design a new way to do something when you don't have all the materials to do it the old way."

Sophia nodded in agreement. "I thought ingenuity meant that, but you really helped me understand it even better. Thank you, Nana Bear."

"We Can Do It!" by J. Howard Miller, 1942

During World War II, many men had to leave their jobs to serve as soldiers. Women, like Rosie the Riveter, displayed ingenuity by successfully working in a variety of jobs that were new to them. Rosie the Riveter became the cultural icon of the worth of the working woman.

Nana Bear laughed loudly as she spied the next float coming around the bend in the road.

Sitting next to a trolley that was rolling around a train track was a gentle-looking boy wearing a red sweater and a very kind smile.

"Welcome to my neighborhood. Would you like to be my neighbor?" asked the boy as he looked down at Beau Bear and Sophia.

"Oh, my, oh, my," smiled Nana Bear. "He was really a great guy, and all the children loved him."

"Who, Nana Bear, who?" asked Beau Bear.

"That is Mr. Rogers," said Nana Bear with great pride, as if she personally knew him.

"Mr. Rogers represents NEIGHBORHOOD."

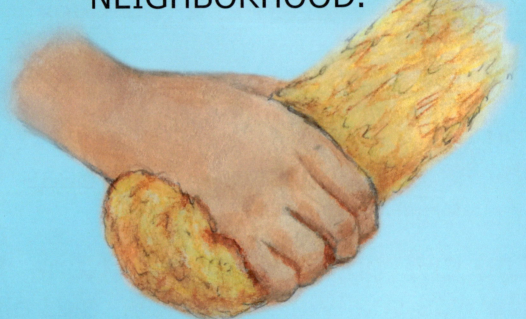

Sophia turned to Beau and whispered, "You are my favorite neighbor. We ride our bikes together and play hide-and-seek a lot. If I need help carrying my things to school, you always help me. You are a good neighbor to me."

Beau Bear's brown, furry face flushed a soft red as his paw nudged Sophia's hand, and she tightly squeezed its velvety softness.

Press Photo published by 1982, public domain.

Fred Rogers hosted an endearing children's television show from 1968 to 2001. His gentle mannerisms and soft voice taught the values of kindness, tolerance, and love of community to children across the globe.

Sounds of lively music filled the air, as the next float came into view.

A young girl with very curly hair smiled as she tap danced with lots of energy.

Nana Bear chuckled. "Now this young lady was a famous dancer and singer when she was a child. When she grew up, she became a public servant and devoted her life to serving her country."

Both Beau Bear and Sophia shouted,

"Who, Nana Bear, Who?"

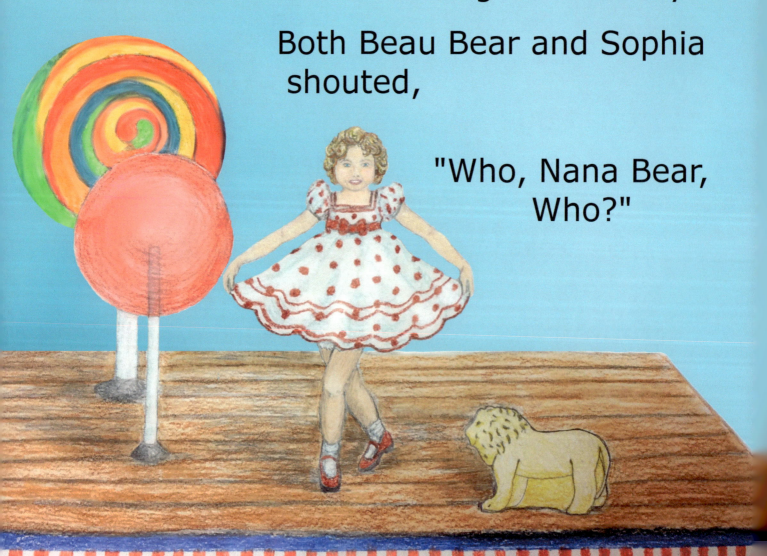

"That person is Shirley Temple Black, and she represents PERFORMANCE."

"Oh," said Beau Bear. "Does that mean to be an actor on the stage?"

Sophia turned her smiling face to Nana Bear to listen, as Nana Bear explained performance to both Sophia and Beau.

"Well, yes, sometimes, but also when you practice and practice your talents and skills, even if it isn't acting on a stage... and you have worked very hard to do the very best job you can do. That is a performance. Your performance can be in many ways, like a nurse, or a teacher, or a biologist, or a computer technician. The important thing is to work hard, practice, and get better each time you perform."

Shirley Temple, 1938, photographers Harry Warnecke and Lee Ekins

Famous as a child actress and singer, Shirley Temple won the hearts of all Americans during the Depression years (1935-1938). As an adult, she served as a Delegate to the United Nations, Ambassador to Ghana and to Czechoslavakia, and as Chief of Protocol of the United States.

Nana Bear turned to Sophia and whispered,

"And now, it's your turn to ride on your float with your family."

The first float in the Family Float Event was slowly coming around the bend in the road. As soon as Sophia spied it, she ran over to join her family float.

Sophia hopped onto the truck, darted behind the curtain, and quickly changed into a red tutu with red sequins. She added a sparkling tiara onto her wavy hair.

Beau Bear and Nana Bear waved as the first entry in the Family Event drove in front of them.

There, in the middle of a cardboard stage and dancing with her ruby red tap shoes and wearing her ruby red dance dress, was Sophia, who represents The Future.

"She looks so happy and confident," sighed Beau as he waved his brown paw until the float was out of sight.

Nana Bear's face was pink and shining. How pleased she was with Sophia's performance.

"Look," exclaimed Beau Bear, as the judge of the Fourth of July parade pinned the winning blue ribbon onto the curtain of the cardboard stage of Sophia's family float.

"Sophia's float won the family award!" Beau Bear's voice cracked a bit with joyful sounds.

Nana Bear hugged Beau tightly in her arms.

The future is always waiting for performances achieved by those patriots who have liberty, adventure, courage, ingenuity, and neighborhood held within their hearts.

About the Author

Bonnie Mackey earned her Ph.D. in Curriculum and Instruction from Texas A&M University. Her teaching experiences include thirteen years at the preschool and elementary levels and nineteen years at the college level. She also has co-authored four professional development books for teachers and librarians.

About the Illustrator

Catherine R. Hamilton owned an art gallery for Central Virginia Artists. She works in various media, with a focus on fused glass and chain maille. She was a regular contributor to *Fired Arts & Crafts* magazine; her work has been published in *Crafts Report* magazine, and in *Art Jewelry.* She is a Delphi Art Glass Festival winner, with work appearing in several of their annual catalogues, and a Fire Mountain Gems and Beads Metal Working Contest winner.

The Nana Bear series is composed of six different books. The theme of each book describes a value as seen through the eyes of a child. Each book is written as a legacy for each of my six granddaughters.

Book One - A Book about Kindness (Katherine)
Book Two - A Book about Imagination (Lorelei)
Book Three - A Book about Patriotism (Sophia)
Book Four - A Book about Puzzles (Annabel)
Book Five - A Book about Nature (Charlotte)
Book Six - A Book about Memories (Ashley)

Made in the USA
Columbia, SC
10 September 2024